# Much Ado About Rutting

## A Planet WLN269 Needs Women Story

Sabrina Cross

Cover Artwork by Anastacia N

Squibble Artwork by Kenzie James

Possum Artwork by Feraichi

Edited By: Writer's Wingman

# Author's Note

While this is a fairly fluffy and short romance novella, there are still a number of topics that you might find distressing. Please take care of yourselves, loves.

This book contains the following: Parental Loss to Cancer, so much sex, somnophilia, double penetration, questionable consent, oral, vaginal, and anal sex.

If you feel I am missing anything please reach out to me at authorsabrinacross@gmail.com and let me know. A complete list can be found at www.sabrinacross.com

# About Planet WLN269:

The United Civilizations of what humans call the Andromeda Galaxy had been fighting a war for centuries—one that had promise of ending soon...until it didn't. It took only one terrorist organization with a biological weapon to take out an entire civilization, leaving behind just one tiny mining colony on the edge of civilized space.

Fifty thousand men, one thousand women were all that was left–a mix that wasn't sustainable. How would these 50,000 men survive without hope for a future, a chance at offspring, or even just companionship?

It could have been the end, were it not for one stubborn woman who refused to allow her brothers to succumb to a life without the possibility of ever finding someone to share their life with.

She was sure her mission to find sentient life would be a lifetime sort of thing—instead, twenty-four hours after launching her search, she found Earth—and accidentally paved the way for the galaxy's most chaotic dating app.

With funding from Earth's governments and a questionable sense of what humans find romantic, the Human Extraterrestrial Liaisons Program (H.E.L.P.) was launched.

Much to the alien's surprise, Earth was full of women ready to leave their planet for anywhere but their current over-populated one. After all, Earth was home to a violent, backward sort of people who happened to have their own male loneliness epidemic—but it was one of their men's own making...

# Chapter 1

## *Rosie*

S*eeking: Human to assist in rutting cycles*

*Requirements: Strong, independent, high sex drive, no desire to spawn or have romantic entanglements.*

I read the bare bones bio again. And again. It is hardly the most romantic thing I've read, but I'm not exactly looking for romance.

"You can't be serious," Betty says from over my shoulder. I shrug her off. Of course, I'm not serious. Except, maybe I am.

The new Human-Extraterrestrial Liaison Program may be exactly what I'm looking for. If I don't think of it like an alien dating app and more of a job site, it's actually quite perfect.

"Rosie, no." I stick my tongue out at my

best friend and ex-husband and go back to ignoring her. "You can't."

I flip back to the program page and read over the details again. The H.E.L.P. site is rather bare bones itself but I guess it would be. It's only existed for a matter of days, and the site has already crashed multiple times from interest.

"What do you think a rut is?" I ask, flipping through the about information going over the sign-up process (which I've done), the mating criteria that leads to matches (which I've gotten), and the stages of courtship (I wonder how much the intergalactic messages are costing the company).

"Breeding season." Betty says, looking up from her phone, where she'd clearly looked it up. "He wants to breed you."

The words send a shudder through me. I was down for a good cream pie, but the thought of actually having kids was enough to put me off my dinner. But the bio did say that his match should have no interest in spawn, which I assume is the alien term for children.

"Pretty sure he doesn't." I say, reading over the benefits list. "Besides, it almost might be worth it for this benefits package.

Free housing, free health care, a stipend to outfit me for space travel and then a settlement once I agree to stay on WLN269."

We both pause to giggle at the ridiculously named planet that sounded like something a preteen boy came up with. Honestly, neither of us is better than a child. It was part of why our marriage fell apart. Neither of us wanted to grow up and be responsible.

That same flaw is part of what has me on the H.E.L.P. website. The settlement would be enough to solve all of my financial problems and give me a truly fresh start. Something I desperately need.

It's been a rough one. After a year of battling brain cancer, I lost my mom in the spring. It was then I realized how bad things had gotten financially. I'd been too consumed with her care to pay attention, but she'd been drowning in debt. There had been just enough from the sale of her house and car to pay her debt off.

Selling the house meant I'd had nowhere to live since I'd moved in with her after my divorce from Betty. Which made it a strange circle of events that found me living in Betty's spare bedroom with her new husband for the last six months.

I am drowning in student loans on a part-time salary while hunting for a position in what may be the worst job market of all time. Betty and Craig are so understanding, but I need to not be living with my ex. And I don't see a way out. H.E.L.P. and Rexus might be my only answer.

"Rosie, don't do anything crazy."

I go back to the bio of the alien I matched with and hit accept.

"Too late."

# Chapter 2

---

## *Rosie*

$S$ *eeking escape from human life. I don't know why you're looking for someone who isn't interested in romantic entanglements, or kids, but I'm here for it. What's your favorite position?*

"You didn't," Craig says, reading over my shoulder. Yet another reason I need out of their house. Betty and Craig lack boundaries. They're great, and I love them both, but boy I could do without their commentary on my every choice.

"What else am I supposed to ask?" Actually, I really wanted to know. I had three months of messages with Rexus before the first trip to WLN269 (snort) would happen and I have no clue what to talk to him about. He made it clear what he was about.

"I don't know. His favorite color?" Craig

ruffles my hair and goes back to the pot of pasta on the stove.

"Maybe next time." Definitely not next time. Who cares what his favorite color is? I want to make sure he's not going to want to fuck me in some impossible position. I'm a tea pot—short and round—not a pretzel.

"How was the interview today?" Craig asks, doing something with the pot of sauce. I don't know. I don't cook.

"I walked out. They're looking for one person to fill three positions at a barely minimum wage salary. Let some twenty-two-year-old do it." The receptionist position I'd interviewed for that morning was really a receptionist, website manager, social media marketer, with a side of security. All for thirty thousand a year. No, thank you.

"Rosie." His voice was tired. I understood. Craig never made me feel unwelcome, and he wasn't threatened by my relationship with Betty, but I was still an extra person in his house. I knew he wanted to see me settled and out of his house almost as much as I did.

"I know, I promise I'm still looking. And if not, in three months I'll be heading off to perv planet and out of your hair." I snap my laptop closed and push away from the table, more annoyed with myself than anything else.

"Rosie, it's not like that." Craig turns around to look at me, but I can't. I just can't.

"I know, hun. I appreciate you." I grab my laptop and drop a kiss on Craig's cheek before heading out of the kitchen and to my bedroom.

# Chapter 3

## *Rosie*

*I do not understand your interest in my position, but I prefer patrolling. Guard jobs do not allow for much activity. My favorite is emergency response, though I dislike the emergencies. I just enjoy the challenge and urgency of them. What is your position?*

My laugh is smothered in my hand so I don't wake up Betty and Craig. Well, that was almost wholesome. I'm a little put off at the idea of him being in law enforcement, but maybe space cops aren't bad. Maybe? Hopefully. Sigh.

I think about answering him, but I don't really want to talk about the fact that the only job I've been able to hold down for the last two years is mixing up bougie coffees at a local coffee shop. I could tell him I'm a writer. It's almost true. I do write. But that's not what I want to do either.

Instead, I give into my inner slut and surf for a photo of a couple doing it doggy. Before I can think better of it, I caption the image with 'this is my favorite position' and hit send.

The message sends at the speed of old-school dial-up. Though thankfully without the demon screeching sound. I wait for the image to load before flipping tabs to look through the digital job boards.

Not that I have any hope. I've been looking for the better part of a year without any luck. I am a pathological student. After high school, I went for my bachelor's in writing. That's where I met Betty. When I told her I wanted to be a doctor in creative writing and literature, she'd supported me. It took me eleven years to get it with me working part-time, going to school full-time, and Betty supporting me financially for most of it.

I'd thought getting my doctorate would be when I finally settled down and settled in. I could get a job, easy. I'd be qualified for anything. Except, Mom got sick and I'd put off looking for a job to care for her. That year of full-time care was the hardest thing

I've ever done and left me numb. And now there was a year gap in my resume.

The doctorate that I so desperately wanted left me overqualified for many jobs in my field. My useless liberal arts degree didn't give me practical skills for other jobs. I was both too smart and too stupid to do anything but make coffee. It's fucking depressing.

The H.E.L.P. tab flashes and I flip over to see a new message from Rexus. An image is loading and my eyes bulge as it begins to come through.

Ok-aaaay then. I grin and settle into bed to see what exactly this spaceman is into.

# Chapter 4

## *Rosie*

I do not know how to describe a rut in a way you can understand. It's an all-consuming need to fuck. To take. There is no satisfying it. We can survive without a mating partner, but it is deeply uncomfortable and extends the duration of the rut if we are unable to get the necessary relief.

So, not unlike ovulating. I think to myself with a small grin. A photo is loading, agonizingly slowly.

"Rosie posy!" Betty sings as she comes into the kitchen. "How do you feel about teaching?"

"Kids or adults?" I'd rather run myself over with a semi-truck than teach small children, and Betty knows it. Not having children was one of the few things we steadfastly agreed upon.

"Adults, of — oh my god! What is that?"

I spin around in my chair to stare open-mouthed at the photo that just finished loading on my screen. Betty leans over my shoulder to get a better look. I think about slapping her away but I can't take my eyes off of the screen.

"Dick pic." I stammer out, trying to take in the image. A very large and scaly light green hand is wrapped around the base of two fully erect penises. They overflow his hand. They resemble normal penises for the most part, except for a weird flare around the base of the head.

"That's..."

"Wow." I finish for her.

"Girl."

"I know." My pussy clenches down at the thought of even one of those cocks filling me. I haven't put any effort into dating in forever, and my last situationship fell in love, fuck, nine months ago, and I haven't had anything but my hand since then.

"Do you think he uses both at once?" Betty asks, leaning closer.

"Both of what?" Craig asks, coming into the kitchen. I slam the laptop shut at the same time Betty jerks upright. We're both red in the face, and when Betty starts giggling, I'm helpless not to join in.

"Our Rosie is about to get very, very lucky." Betty says, crossing the kitchen to greet her husband with a kiss. She whispers something in his ear, and Craig's eyebrows rise as he looks at me.

"I wanna see."

"Nope." I shove to my feet and grab my laptop off the table. "Bye."

And I run for it. I want to investigate that photo some more. Without an audience.

# Chapter 5

## *Rosie*

"Is there some way to get my IUD replaced while I'm there?" I ask as the doctor finishes her pelvic exam. "It's only a year old but I'd hate to have no way to get it replaced."

"Their medical team will have everything you could need." She assures me, then shoves back away from the table and gestures for me to sit up. "Everything looks great. Assuming there's nothing in your other tests, this time next week you'll be heading to the moon."

I am practically vibrating in anticipation as I get dressed and make my way out of the H.E.L.P. medical offices. I can hardly believe how fast the last three months have gone. Between the long-term substitution teacher placement at the local community college and sexting with Rexus, it has been the best three months in recent history.

The school had offered me a long-term placement for next year, but I turned it down, much to Betty's dismay and Craig's confusion. Sure, it would have paid well enough to get a small one-bedroom and keep me on Earth, but honestly, I'm excited to meet Rexus.

He's funny, in a gruff way. He's sexy as fuck once you get used to the green scales. And the male can dirty talk like no one's business.

Plus, there was the reason I've never told anyone. If I can pay off debt and don't have to worry about that anymore, I can finally focus on the book I've wanted to write my entire life. It's a tempting lure. Almost as tempting as Rexus' dicks.

I know Betty is confused and concerned, but I don't want to tell her about the book. She's listened to my excuses for over a decade, and I don't want to disappoint her if I fail. She believed in me when everyone else said I was being silly and frivolous. I don't want to get her hopes up only to let her down again.

"Well?" She asks as I meet her outside the clinic.

"They said I should have the results tomorrow. If I'm deemed healthy enough, they'll make the first payment."

Which meant shopping. The climate on WLN269 is apparently livable but cold, and as a native Alabama girl, I'm not outfitted for cold. It's honestly the biggest turnoff of this whole thing.

"We'll start ordering your clothes tonight!" Betty loves shopping. I hate her a little for it. But she's right. We have to start ordering clothes ASAP because there's no way we're finding the right winter gear in Alabama. Especially not in my size.

"Yay?" I say as we reach the car and I slide into the passenger seat.

"Hush, it'll be fun. We'll get you something slutty to make it fun."

"You realize I don't have to seduce him, right? We know the score. It's just sex."

Betty joins me in the car and starts it up. I fight the urge to check my phone to see if there's a new message from Rexus.

"The something slutty is for you. I give zero fucks if he ever sees it." Betty shakes her head as she puts the car in drive and pulls into traffic. "I have failed you if you don't understand the point of slutty underwear."

"Bitch, I'm the one who explained it to you."

"Oh, right." She gives me a side-eye and a frown. "But you seem to have forgotten."

I ignore that. It's not like I've had a lot of reasons to wear slutty undies. Or the money to invest in them. But she might have a point. The stipend they're giving me is to outfit me for my new life off planet. Some slutty little undies are just the right thing for the life I'm heading into.

# Chapter 6

## *Rexus*

I have regrets.

They strangle me as I make my way to Headquarters, where the Planet WL-N269 H.E.L.P. offices reside. I should not have listened to my comrades and signed up for a human companion. I do not want or need the distraction.

But my comrades were also right that my ruts were getting worse and it was taking longer to get over them. And being gone was a strain on my unit. Something I never wanted to be. Since the galaxy went silent, my unit was all I had.

Except now, I guess, I have a human. What was I thinking?

Village 22, where I reside, is half a cycle transport from Headquarters. I could have made the journey yesterday and been present when the ships landed, but I hadn't wanted to disrupt the schedule more than I had to.

This was a terrible idea. But it is too late, and I'm stuck with the human for the foreseeable future. Once the trial period ends, I'll just explain to her I've changed my mind and it isn't a good fit. Then I'll send her on her way. There has to be another answer to my ruts.

It's not that I don't like the human. Rosie is amusing, and I've taken great pleasure in our communication. If she is as fun in real life as she is via messaging, we'll do okay for her time here.

I'm almost looking forward to a rut. Which is not something I've ever experienced before. But it's been a long while since I've sated my need on someone else. There is only so much pleasure one can derive from themselves.

The mid-day sun is high as I pull into Headquarters and make my way to the human waiting area. They are here. I can hear the chatter of female voices, but I can't make out the words. At first, I think my translator implant has failed but then I realize there is too much going on for it to translate properly.

Already my head hurts. Does Rosie talk this much? I hope not. I do not want a house full of chatter. Having her there will already be disruptive enough.

I check in at the desk and enter the offices, ready to find my human and leave. Again, we could stay the night at Headquarters, but I want to be home in my own bed. It makes me anxious to be away from my post for so long.

Scanning over the crowd, I spot her immediately. She looks exactly like the photos she sent, perhaps a bit fluffier with a less defined shape. Which is a shame. I am rather fond of the shape she had. Her hair is long and light as it hangs around her shoulders. Her round face is pulled down into a frown as she looks at something on her table.

She doesn't notice me as I reach her table. Instead, she maintains her focus on the pad in front of her. It's filled with black markings of some sort. Drawing? Writing? I am not certain.

"Hello Rosie." The human jumps and whips her head up to look at me. Then her eyes go down. There's a long moment where she looks me over before her eyes meet mine again. This time they're hot.

Interesting.

24

# Chapter 7

## *Rosie*

Rexus is a male of few words. Very few. Like, maybe a couple of dozen words during the multi-hour trip from the landing pad to his home. At first, I'd tried to make conversation.But he was having none of it.

Well, he had said no relationship and no feelings. I guess I didn't think that meant no talking either. I roll my eyes and turn my focus back to the scenery. If you can call it that.

I'd much rather stare at Rexus himself, but he'd told me to stop doing that hours ago. He was tall, well over six feet. He was nearly as broad as I am round, but his size is all lean muscle. He wears a pair of low-slung brown pants and a black leathery jacket. His chest is bare under the jacket, and it shows off exactly how jacked he is. And every inch of him is covered in scales.

His head is very reptilian, which seemed strange when I first saw his picture, but it oddly suits him. As does the short tail that stops about his knees. I wonder how much control he has over that tail...

I stop thinking about the male next to me and focus outside the window. The planet is mostly flat and brown. Hard dirt with mounds here and there where I imagine the mines are. We pass a number of villages but do not slow down or stop in any of them. I have the vague impression of brown and grey and glass and nothing else. It's far less exciting than I expected.

I have a million questions I'd like to ask, but I don't bother trying to ask Rexus. He has two modes: clipped answers or grunts. Neither of which are very helpful, and the former just pisses me off.

If I wanted an asshole who didn't want to talk to me, I could have dated any man back on Earth. This male's dicks better live up to my expectations, is all I gotta say.

The sun has gone down by the time we pull up to a gated village. We're waved through the gates and only traverse inside for a short time before he pulls into some sort of garage.

"Is this it?" I ask, unable to help myself. He grunts, and I want to stab him with my pen. He opens the top of the transport and jumps out with an agility that annoys me. More when it kind of turns me on.

I don't move. There's no way I can hop out like that, and I don't know how the door works. Rexus sighs but comes to open the side for me. I reach for my bags, but he gets to them first, lifting both suitcases and my large duffel bag with an ease that sends my pulse fluttering.

"There are no multi-room domiciles available at the moment. I was able to get you a domicile on my floor so you'll be nearby but have you own space." I'm a little shocked at the idea of having my own space. I hadn't put much thought into sleeping arrangements but figured if I was there to fuck, we'd probably share a bed.

I guess not.

I have questions that need answers, but I don't push him as he leads me from the garage into the building and into a sleek lift that takes us up to the third floor. There are two units on the floor, so it would just be us. That was something, I guess.

"That's me," He points to the left of the lift before turning us to the door on the right. It's a sliding door with a panel. He keys something in and then lifts my hand to the plate. It warms under my touch before beeping quietly and sliding open with a small whoosh.

"This is your domicile." I walk inside, not at all sure what to expect. It certainly isn't the outrageously pink, grey, and glass space I'm facing. It's just...so much pink.

Rexus presses by me with my bags, which knocks me out of my shock. The door slides shut behind me, and I jump a little and try to take in more than just the decor.

To the left, there is what looks like a small kitchen area with appliances I cannot begin to guess how they work. I only identify it by the small square metal table. To the right, there is a low-slung couch covered in fuzzy pink pillows and blankets. Behind it is a glass wall that looks out over the planet's surface.

There's an alcove with three doors off of it. That's where Rexus is heading. I follow.

"Showers," he points to the door to the left.

"Storage," he points to the door straight back.

"Bedroom," he steps back to allow me to go into the bedroom first. I press my hand to the panel, and it slides open.

# Chapter 8

## *Rosie*

My first impression is pink. More pink than was in the living room. At least that was broken up by metal tables and the black of the couch. But here it's just all pink.

Pink carpet takes up most of the floor. Pink bedding. Pink pillows. Pink walls. Pink. Pink. Pink.

It isn't until my second pass that I spot the small grey thing on the bed. It's curled up small into a ball, and I think it's another pillow at first. Until it twitches.

I step forward to investigate and sense Rexus stepping into the room behind me. I barely register him putting the suitcases down on the floor by the dresser as I reach for the little fluff ball.

My hand nearly makes contact when it

uncurls, and I find myself face to face with a possum. I scream and jump back. It screams and falls down onto its side to play dead.

Same, possum, same.

"W-why is there a possum on my bed?"

Rexus looks between me and the possum before he shrugs. "It's a cat. Human women like cats."

He looks discomforted by my questioning, and I have no clue why. I'm too busy trying to hold it together.

There is a fucking possum on my bed, and the male I'm here to fuck says it's a cat. A fucking cat. Thankfully, it isn't, as I'm seriously allergic to cats.

"I thought you might like the company." He shrugs again and shoves his hands into his pockets. I realize this was him trying to do something nice. "I'll be busy on patrol much of the time."

"Oh," I still don't have words. I have no clue what I'm going to do with a possum. I know nothing about them besides the fact that they supposedly don't carry rabies, eat trash, and play dead. But it's a gift, so I'll do my best to keep the rodent alive. "That was thoughtful of you."

"Yeah, well," he shrugs again, and I get

the feeling he is deeply uncomfortable with the gesture. I try to move on. "I'll leave you to get settled."

He starts out of the room and then stops to give me a once over I don't quite understand. He reaches forward to grab something off of the dresser. After looking at it for a moment, he hands it to me.

"I'm programmed in. Message me if you need anything."

And then he's gone. And I'm alone on an alien planet. Alone with something that looks like a tablet had a baby with a black-berry and a possum sleeping on my bed.

What. The. Fuck?

# Chapter 9

## *Rexus*

I fled. I'm not ashamed to admit it. Well, not to myself at any rate.

What was a male to do when the woman he courted specifically to fuck was standing there all cute and smelling good? She was here for my ruts, not for me to throw over my shoulder anytime I wanted.

So, I did the only sane thing a male in my position could do. I ran back to my apartment to settle my nervous system before I burst into her space and pinned her to the bed.

The hot look she gave me at Headquarters flashes through my mind, and I try not to read into it. It is good she finds me attractive, right? She isn't afraid of me, as some of the humans had seemed. She seems open to my touch.

I close that train of thought down. Not going there. Not yet.

My rut is due soon. It isn't clockwork, like some are. It's a hormonal cycle that can be sped up or slowed down with certain stimuli or management tools. But her presence is going to be a test of will.

I tear off my coat and throw it over the chair before I begin to pace my domicile as I try to shove the rising heat down. I had not anticipated wanting her outside of a rut, but the attraction had been instantaneous. I close my eyes and tip my head back, trying not to think of the messages we've exchanged during the courting period. The teasing. The photos. Oh fuck, the photos.

My groan echoes through my domicile as I try to will my cocks back down. It's almost a relief when my communicator beeps. I'm technically off-duty for the next two days so I can get the human settled in, but we're always on call in case of emergency.

*We should do a test run.*

*You know, to make sure everything works.*

I stare at the words, not sure I comprehend the meaning. She can't possibly mean...

*A test run?*

*Yeah, I've never fucked anyone with two dicks before. Like, how does that even work?*

Between one heartbeat and the next, I'm out of my domicile and across the hall. My cocks are straining against my pants. I knock once and brace my arms on the door frame to keep myself from letting myself in.

It only takes a second before the door slides open and exposes Rosie. She looks different than she had before. The puffiness must have been a result of her outerwear because she's all rounded curves now. She wears some sort of cut-off bottoms that show off thick legs and a dark top that barely contains her breasts. I want to bite the curve of them.

"You want to know how my cocks work?" I say, my voice low.

"You know, for science." Rosie runs a hand along the bare expanse of belly, and my eyes lock in on the movement.

"Anything for science."

# Chapter 10

## *Rosie*

Rexus launches himself off the doorframe and into my apartment. The door slides shut behind him as he wraps his arms around my hips and lifts me. I shriek and tell him to put me down before he hurts himself.

"Don't worry, pet. I can handle you." He sinks his teeth into the curve of my neck and I writhe against him.

Yeah, this is definitely the best idea I've had recently. Get it out of the way so we know if we're even any good together. No point in being awkward and weird around each other when we could just fuck it out.

A conclusion I came to about thirty seconds after he left me alone in my bedroom. I'd caught the possum up in a blanket and locked it into the bathroom before changing into some silky shorts and matching cropped cami. I wanted there to be no doubt about what I was after.

Rexus clearly got my point. I laugh as he tosses me onto the bed. I've barely stopped bouncing before he's on me. His long nose nuzzles into my neck, and he licks my skin. I gasp and arch into him.

He lost his coat before coming over, so there's no barrier between me and his torso. I run my hands over his cool skin. His scales are softer than I expected, and the muscle under them is firm. I want to wrap my legs around him and ride him through both of our clothes from underneath.

Twelve months of sexual frustration and three months of teasing messages have coalesced into an impossible need. My pussy is already clenching around nothing, and I'm about to start begging when Rexus moves down to lick my pointed nipple through my top. His teeth close around the point and I arch into him.

"Fuck yes," I moan, wrapping a hand around one of his horns.

"This won't be gentle," Rexus warns me, pushing my shirt up until he can lick at my peaked nipple.

"Did I ask for gentle?" The words seem

to unlock him. Rexus pushes up and off of me. He grabs my hips and flips me over. I land on my belly with a squeak, but before I can even adjust to the new position, he's yanking my shorts off.

For a moment I'm worried he's just going to go for it. Especially when I hear his belt clink and zipper go down. But then he's back on me. His broad hands grip my ass and the tops of my thighs, and he's spreading me wide. I nearly jump when his tongue darts out to lick a streak between my spread lips and cheeks.

I yelp when he pauses to circle his tongue around my ass. The touch is unexpected. Rexus quickly moves down to delve into my pussy. I fist my hands into the bedding as he presses deep. His tongue goes deeper than any human man's has ever gone. He's practically flicking against my cervix, and I can't help but squirm.

"You taste delicious." Rexus says, pulling out and moving down to flick his deft tongue against my clit. "Tell me you're ready for me, human."

"So ready," I moan out, wiggling back into his touch. I whimper when he pulls away, but he's there again, firm against my ass as he presses one of his cocks against me.

I'd wondered if he would use both at once, but I can feel the second cock sliding against my ass as he pushes forward, inside. I nearly ask him but then he's thrusting forward and words leave me. Oxygen leaves me. Everything but the feel of his massive cock inside of me is gone.

"Oh, my god," I pant out, dropping my head onto my arms. "So good."

Rexus chuckles, and his grip on my hips tightens as he starts to move. His cock slides in deep and stretches me so good, even as his other cock slides against my puckered hole, teasing the rear entrance with every movement.

My legs shake as Rexus fucks me. Sweat beads across my skin, and my breath comes in pants as I take everything he gives me. I want to ask him to fuck my ass, but I'm worried that it'll offend him. Maybe that's not something aliens did. So I keep quiet because if he stops fucking me right now I'm going to cry.

The weird flare under the head of his penis rubs inside of me just right and catches on my g-spot with every thrust, and it takes practically no time before I'm riding the edge of orgasm.

"Yes, please. Harder."

"So the little human likes it rough?" Rexus says, thrusting harder. His grip on my hips is almost painful, but it's the good kind of pain that adds that little something extra to the pleasure. "Tell me, human, how much more can you take?"

Honestly, I'm not sure. I'm on the edge and prepared to beg as it is. My muscles are straining to keep it together, and I'm one good thrust away from an orgasm. But that doesn't stop the brat in me from issuing a challenge.

"Anything you've got."

# Chapter 11

## *Rexus*

Fuck, she's perfect. I know she's close. I can feel the tension in her body and in the way her tight little pussy clenches my cock. But if she's not going to admit it, I'm not going to make it easy on her.

Might as well see how much she can take right now. Once my rut hits, there won't be any stopping. I have no control in that state, and it can last anywhere from hours to days. The literature on humans suggested they might not be able to handle a full rut, but the woman in front of me doesn't seem like she'll back down.

I grip her hips tight and thrust harder, grinding deep at the end of every thrust before pulling back. I'm getting close. Her pussy is so tight and hot around my cock that even the smallest movements are a shock of sensation.

"Fuck, fuck, fuck." Rosie chants the word as she goes rigid in front of me. She's so tense I worry about breaking her, but something gives and it's all over for me. Her pussy clenches around me in rhythmic pulses that squeeze my cock just right. I jerk forward and freeze deep in her pussy as lightning shoots through me. My cock empties into her with heavy spurts of cum that leaves me feeling tense and edgy.

It is possible to achieve full relief with one cock, but tonight, one won't be enough. My second cock is rock hard and throbbing against Rosie's spread ass. I could be in her second hole in one thrust, but her reaction to my tongue tells me she wouldn't welcome the invasion.

The human slumps down onto the bed. Well, that won't do. I pull out of her with a wet sound and flip her over until she's on her back. I need more. I need back inside.

I shove her legs up to her chest and spread her wide. She makes a slightly disgruntled sound, but I don't stop until the tip of my second cock is pressed against her opening.

"Tell me no if you don't want it." I

thrust forward in tiny little thrusts that just tease the tip to my ridge. The ridge is hyper-sensitive and it feels amazing as it slides against her soaked heat.

"Fuck me already." Rosie demands, her arms coming up to wrap around her legs to hold herself open for me.

So. Fucking. Perfect.

I do what she says and fuck her. I slide deep with one hard thrust. Her release has made her so wet, and the sounds are indecent as I move inside of her. I grip her hips as I move and keep my eyes locked on where my body invades her. Human anatomy is beautiful. I've been with multiple species, and they're all different, but not all of them are as pleasing to look at.

A dark bud peeks out at me, and I poke at it. Rosie goes tense and lets out a high-pitched squeak. My eyes flick to her face. She's thrown her head back and is panting. Her face is pink and glistens from effort. It's almost as beautiful as the cunt squeezing me tight.

I poke the bud again and then press down when Rosie makes more of those delicious sounds. Are all humans so vocal? I could get used to all of the verbal feedback.

When I press my thumb against the

bud and circle it, Rosie goes tight with a moan. Clearly, the bud is the source of great pleasure. I grin as I continue my movements.

"How you doing?" I ask, pressing harder on her bud as I thrust deep inside of her. She grits her teeth, but her eyes meet mine in a glare. I love her fire.

"Fuck you."

"I believe I'm too busy fucking you, thanks." It's hard to keep the words sounding dismissive and teasing as I move inside of her. Her movements are causing my ridge to twist inside of her as I thrust, and it's almost too much to take.

"Shut up," the words are harsh, but she's laughing as she says them. The laughter is my undoing. The way her soft body is shaking under me is just too much to handle.

I move my thumb against her bud in quick movements as I lean forward and grip her splayed thigh with my other hand. I thrust hard and fast, pulling out until my ridge slides against her entrance and push deep until I hit the firm end of her cunt.

"So fucking good," I say through clenched teeth as she trembles beneath me. Her reply is a moan. "Scream for me."

I thrust deep one last time and she breaks. Her body tenses, and she does what I demand. She screams for me.

# Chapter 12

## *Rosie*

P lanet WLN269 is boring.

Other than the absolutely mind-blowing sex my first night on planet, it's been a rather dull week. Rexus didn't exactly fuck and run, but the aftercare was seriously lacking. A damp rag and a glass of water before a quiet exit was hardly enough for fucking me until my legs stopped working.

Then again, he'd been clear on the 'no feelings' rule from the start, so I guess I couldn't expect more from him. Other than coming over to teach me how the food ordering system worked, Rexus hasn't been by since my first night.

I've thought more than once about inviting him over for another round, but that felt needy. I wasn't here to be a regular fuck buddy. I was here to get out of debt, write my novel, and take care of his mating season. That was it.

So what if my pussy clenched at the memory of how it felt to have his cock inside of me regularly? Who cares that it was hands down the best sex of my life? Big deal if I wake up every morning wet from dirty dreams about that sex?

Not the point.

I force myself to pay attention to the communicator in front of me. I would have preferred my laptop, but there wasn't a compatible charging method yet, so I was stuck with alien technology. Writing a novel on a tablet wasn't the plan, but it beats longhand, I guess.

You'd think it'd be easy to write a book when on a literal alien planet, but so far, it's been as slow going as it was on Earth. Maybe I wasn't meant for writing? Not everyone is. Nearly everyone says they'd like to write a book one day, but so few actually do. Maybe I'm just meant to read and analyze them.

No. Nope.

I shut that train of self-defeating thought down. I did not spend eleven years in school learning the ins and outs of the written word only to give up now.

Maybe I just need a change of scenery. The walls of my apartment are starting to feel like a prison. Technically, I'm allowed outside so long as I stay within the village gates. But I feel like a zoo animal out there. All the trouble of getting a neural implant to translate all languages and I can't even get anyone to say hello. What a waste.

I'd understood I was coming to a planet of males, but I had imagined myself making friends with some of them. I hadn't imagined being isolated in my apartment all day every day just waiting for Rexus to get horny enough to fuck me.

Which he didn't seem interested in doing again anytime soon.

A knock on the door startles me. Pickles the possum, who had been chilling on a pillow on the table, jumps up and then goes limp. Drama queen. Honestly, she was pretty good company, if you could get past the creepy little hands and worm-like tail. She listened to all of my inane thoughts and didn't judge me. Much.

The person, who I'm assuming is Rexus, knocks again. With a roll of my eyes, I push away from the table and cross to the door. Oh look, I was right. Rexus stands there in a pair of low-slung camo pants and sturdy work boots. And nothing else. I don't mind, it's a nice view.

"What's up?" I ask, stepping back for him to come inside.

"Up?" He looks toward the ceiling and I fight back a giggle. I guess even universal translators can't make sense of some phrases.

"What can I do for you?" The door slides shut behind Rexus, and I struggle not to fidget. I haven't spent much time with him at all since I arrived, and despite him fucking me every which way, I'm a little nervous.

"My rut is coming." He stops looking around the apartment and meets my eyes. "I wanted to prepare you."

"Oh," I'm not sure what else to say to that. Thanks for warning me. Wanna have dinner?

The situation is strange. He's sponsoring my existence on this planet, but I know nothing about him really. And he knows nothing about me. We're both just here for sex. Which, okay, don't get me wrong, it's really, really good sex. But part of me wonders if this is sustainable long-term.

Doesn't matter. I've made my bed, and now I'll sleep in it. Alone.

"I'm sorry but I won't have much control or sense once it hits. I do not want to scare or hurt you." He doesn't break eye contact, and I fight the urge to squirm.

"Are you likely to?"

"I hope not. I've never been with a human during a rut before. I don't know what your body is capable of handling. But I'm not always in control of myself."

I'd done research on ruts when we matched, and I understood it was a breeding cycle that could get pretty intense. But, as much as he was trying to warn me, I wasn't worried. It might be insane and misplaced, but there was something deep inside of me that trusted Rexus not to seriously hurt me. Not in ways I didn't enjoy.

And if I'm wrong? Well, that was something we'd deal with if it came to it. There was no turning back now.

"Gotcha." I shrug and dig my hands into my sweatpants pockets. It drags the waistband down, and Rexus' gaze is drawn to the small strip of skin between my pants and sweater. He may not want me, but he wanted my body. There was no denying that.

"Anything else?" I don't want him to go, but I don't understand what is happening. I am at risk of doing something crazy like throwing myself at him, and he'd been clear that isn't what our relationship is about.

"Guess not." He looks around the apartment again and hooks his thumbs through his belt loops. "Getting settled in okay?"

"Yeah, I'm good."

"Good." There's a long moment of silence before he gives me a nod and heads out of the apartment.

Well, that was fun.

# Chapter 13

## *Rosie*

I'm lying on the couch with the communicator waiting on a message from Betty when the door slides open without warning. I sit up to yell at whoever just broke into my apartment when I see Rexus. He's standing in the open door, his chest heaving. He's again not wearing a shirt and just low slung pants, but his belt buckle is already undone and hanging open at his waist.

His hands are on his buttons. Oh fuck, is this it?

"Rexus?" I set the communicator aside and get to my feet. I've barely found my balance before he's across the room and picking me up. He throws me over his shoulder and heads into the bedroom.

I let out a surprised squeal and grab his shoulders. "No, put me down!"

A second later I get my wish when he throws me onto the bed. I barely have time to catch my breath before he's on me. He buries his face in my neck and inhales. There's a low rumble in his chest.

"You smell good enough to eat." I really hope that is a phrase and that he doesn't intend to eat me. They wouldn't put human-eating aliens in the program, right?

Before I go down that spiral of crazy, he licks a long swipe up my neck and hums like he's savoring my flavor. Nope. Uh-uh.

Before I can object, he's shoving at my pants, trying to get them down while he's still propped between my legs. His tongue is doing insane things to my neck, and I flash hot when his teeth scrape against my skin.

Well, he did warn me he'd be a little out of his mind. Clearly, he's also lacking some critical thinking skills. I push on his chest until he pushes up to his forearms. I wriggle my way out from under him. He tries to stop me, but I roll off the bed until I land on the floor in a heap. Not my best plan, but we were getting nowhere with his method.

"Pants off." I demand. I've been lonely

and horny for days. No way I was missing my chance for a little male contact and taking the edge off. I wriggle out of my leggings and hoodie while Rexus fights with his boots and pants.

I'm back on the bed in nothing but my socks by the time he gets his clothes off. I am about to take them off when he pounces. He spreads me wide and buries his face against my pussy. There is no finesse in his movements as he devours me. It's wet and sloppy as he flicks his tongue through my folds, into me, and against my clit. There's no rhythm or reason to his movements, and I can't figure out what's coming next. It shouldn't work as well as it does, but within minutes I'm wet and panting.

"Please," I beg, gripping the sheets for dear life and tilting my hips to get him where I need him. There's no relief. He dives his tongue inside me and groans against me. The vibration is an evil tease.

When he groans and pulls away, I nearly cry. Instead, I let out a startled yelp as he grabs my hips and flips me over. I'm ass up, head down in moments and, before I can even adjust to the position, he's there. Driving into me with one of his cocks.

My eyes roll back as I feel it stretching me wide. He groans and grips my hips before setting a brutal, punishing pace. His second cock is between my legs, sliding through my folds and slamming against my clit with every thrust.

"Fuck, fuck, fuck, fuck, fuck." I chant the word as my world tightens down to Rexus and his two cocks and the way they're working my body in ways I've never been fucked before. My chest aches as I try to catch my breath through the brutal pounding.

It could have been a moment or it could have an hour, time loses all meaning as I grip the sheets and just try to breathe through it. It's so good. It's too much. I whine as pressure builds inside of me.

Rexus thrusts forward again and this time, when his cock slams home and the second one knocks against my clit, it's all over. I explode into orgasm with a scream. My eyes clench shut, and suddenly I understand the concept of being fucked so good you see stars.

I go limp beneath him, but he's not done. He follows me down until he's stretched over me, between my limply splayed thighs. His cock continues to move inside me. His second cock is trapped between my body and the bed and is applying almost constant pressure against my clit.

Whines and moans fall from my lips as I try to escape. It's too much. But my position doesn't allow for leverage. I'm so spent I don't have the energy to do anything but take it as he continues to work my spent pussy and overstimulated clit in quick, short thrusts.

My entire body shakes as I come again. The clench of my pussy on his cock is almost painful in its intensity. Rexus drives deep and stills above me. His cock twitches and jerks inside of me as he fills me.

I go limp when he pulls out, thankful for the reprieve. My entire body is lax and limp as I lie splayed on the bed with his cum pooling inside of me.

"Oh fuck," I groan as I feel his second cock sliding inside of me. It's harder now, I'm tense and tight, but it doesn't stop Rexus from working his cock inside of me with short thrusts. "I can't. Not yet."

Rexus just growls and yanks my hips up until I'm resting on my knees with my torso spread against the bed. With a final thrust, he's buried deep inside of me. This time he doesn't pound my pussy but grinds into me with slow circles of his hips. He's so deep he's grinding the tip of his cock against my cervix. I claw at the sheets at the intense sensation. It's unlike anything I've felt before, and it's so much. Too much.

This time, orgasm doesn't explode through me. It creeps up in waves of sensation that wash over my body before crashing into me. I'm gasping for air and drowning in pleasure as Rexus continues to work my body until tears fall down my face and I'm so spent I can't keep my eyes open.

When Rexus finally pulls free of my body, it's followed by a gush of cum. It runs down my pussy, but before it can fall to the bed, he's there. He uses his fingers to scoop it up and finger fuck it back into me.

I let out a feeble moan and crash flat against the bed. My legs are hanging over the end of the bed, but I can't move. I've never been so fucked out in my entire life. Rexus pulls his fingers free of my body, but I can't be bothered to move.

He's moving around the bed, but I lose track of him as I fall asleep.

# Chapter 14

## *Rosie*

"Wake up, little one." I groan and try to snuggle deeper into the pillow I'm hugging. Every fiber of my body aches. My pussy has a pulse of its own. The room reeks of sweat and sex.

Rexus is already buried deep inside of me with his second cock pressed between my legs and nestled between my lips. Had he even pulled out from the last time? Did I fall asleep with him fucking me?

Honestly, I have no clue. I don't know how much time has passed since Rexus burst into my apartment but it's been non-stop fucking with short breaks for sleeping. Emphasis on the short. I am a kind of tired I've never experienced before in my life. Grad school had nothing on Rexus in a rut.

Rexus is curled up behind me with his cock inside of me and one hand cupping my boob. If you would have asked me a week ago if it was possible to sleep with a cock inside of you, I'd have said no way in hell. Now, I would take any sleep I could get.

I moan when Rexus begins to move his hips in slow, short thrusts. The flare under his head scrapes my insides and sets of little aftershocks that have me whimpering into my pillow.

"No more," I whine, mumbling the words into the fabric under my face. "Can't take anymore."

His hand shifts to roll my nipple between his fingers and I arch against him. Every part of my body is sensitive and over-stimulated. How much longer can this go on? How much longer can I keep taking his cocks before I lose my mind.

"You can take it, little one." He thrusts again and rolls his hips while buried deep. I clench around him and whimper at the sensation. "This little pussy was made for my cocks. You're taking them so well."

As if to prove his point, he picks up speed and I can't help but angle my hips to take him better. My orgasm is already building at the lazy fuck. It doesn't seem possible that I can still orgasm. You'd think my body would be dead at this point.

"Are you going to come for me, hmm?" He drops his hand from my breast to cup my mound. His fingers press his cock tighter to my clit where it rubs the swollen, sensitive bud with every movement. I whimper and clench around him. "Oh yeah, I love the way you squeeze my cocks. So perfect."

He nuzzles into my neck and licks at my skin. I shudder, knowing my neck is a mix of sweat and saliva. He seems to enjoy the taste of my skin since he keeps tasting me. Gross, but to each their own, I guess.

His teeth close over my shoulder and I shudder. It seems to be what Rexus is looking for because suddenly the slow movements are gone and he's slamming into me with force. I cry out as my orgasm hits with brutal force.

There's a moment of relief when Rexus tenses and finishes but I know it's not over. It's never over. Cum coats my legs as he pulls out. He's stopped trying to keep it all inside of me. There's just too much. It coats us both as he shifts until his other cock is buried inside of me.

"Such a good little cunt." He says, moving up to cup my breast again. He doesn't start moving so I allow myself to drift off. He'll be waking me up again soon enough.

# Chapter 15

## *Rexus*

The tight clutch of Rosie's cunt wakes me up but for the first time in days I don't feel the insatiable drive to move. I'm laying on my back with Rosie sprawled on top of me. One cock is pressed inside of her, the other is caught tight between our bodies.

I groan as I move and feel the soreness in every muscle of my body. I can hardly shift without the tense ache rocking through me. The room reeks of sex and sweat and I can feel the dried cum all over me.

Rosie groans a weak 'no' as I slide out of her body with a messy pop. Cum pours out of her and adds to the mess between us. My face screws up in disgust. I've always hated this part. Coming back to sense after days of rut always leaves me feeling pained and unclean. I hate the loss of self that comes with rut and wondering what I've done while insensible is a maddening experiment in futility.

I run my hand down the human's silky back and cup her ass. It overflows my hand and the rounded softness stirs actual desire. It's not like the overwhelming heat of the rut but something quieter, softer. And unwanted.

She held up against my rut better than I expected but I hadn't brought her here for anything else. I don't do relationships and trying only ends up in pain.

For a brief moment, Seela flashes to mind but I push it down. I don't want her here. Not now, not while I'm in bed with someone else. Not ever, really. There's no point in thinking about someone who's long gone.

I gently slide out from under Rosie, careful not to wake her. She barely shifts as I climb out of bed. Just wraps herself around the pillow. I stand by the bed and watch her for a moment. She's so soft and round and rosy. A part of me wants to wrap myself around her again and enjoy the press of her against me.

But then my eyes catch the space between her legs and guilt slams through me. What had been all soft and pink the first time we were together is an angry red and swollen. A primal satisfaction wells up as I see my cum leaking out of her clenched hole. The trail of it lands on her leg, which is sticky with previous loads.

I did this to her. Disgust overtakes satisfaction as I think about the abuse I'd heaped on her body to make her so visibly sore. When I brush my fingers gently over the red flesh, Rosie groans and shifts away from me. What kind of monster am I?

Pulling away, I grab a blanket from the heap of them on the floor and drape it over her. I gather my pants and boots from the floor and slink out of her bedroom to leave her to her rest. I need a shower and to figure out how to make it up to the human.

# Chapter 16

## *Rosie*

My everything hurts. I shift and groan as my tense muscles pull. My pussy is throbbing and a kind of sore I've never imagined. I'm not even sure I can close my legs anymore.

That's when I realize Rexus isn't there. I'm completely alone in bed.

I don't like the sinking sensation that comes with that realization. We were both clear about what this is. Neither of us are looking for love or a relationship. So what is this hollow sensation all about?

The door slides open, and I clench the blanket around me. Which is ridiculous because we've been naked and fucked for days straight. He's seen me from pretty much every imaginable angle.

Rexus draws up short just inside the door. "You're awake."

I nod. My throat is dry and aches. I'm so dehydrated it isn't even funny. There's no way I'm moving from this bed until I've had at least a gallon of water. While I'd managed a couple of bathroom breaks during the fuck-a-thon, there hadn't been time for anything else.

"You were out for a while. I was beginning to worry. I brought things." He adjusts the bundle in his arms. When he pulls a metal bottle free, I could sob. Except, I can't because I'm pretty sure even my tear ducts are dried out right now.

I struggle into a sitting position and gladly take the bottle from him. The blanket pools at my waist as I sip at the water. I'm too tired, and modesty has gone out the window. The water is cool, and I fight not to gulp it. But it's been days since I've had anything, and I know enough to know that's a bad idea.

"We'll have to plan better before my next rut," Rexus says, setting the rest of his bundle down on the foot of the bed. It looks like a change of sheets. "Your needs were ignored."

I groan, unwilling to even consider another rut at the moment. I'm still lying in the mess of the previous one. My skin itches with dried fluids, and every muscle aches.

"How often do they happen?" I swear to fuck, if he tells me it's monthly like a period; I'm getting on the next shuttle home, debt be damned.

"Usually a couple of times a year." He steps back and puts his hands in his pockets. He's once again in a pair of low-slung, belted pants and his boots. His scales are shiny, like he just got out of the shower.

Ugh. What I wasn't willing to do for a shower right now. Unfortunately, I don't think my legs are strong enough to hold me yet.

"So we have time," I say with a lack of enthusiasm. The last few days have taught me that no matter how high my sex drive is, there is such a thing as too much sex.

"Yes." He looks awkward and uncomfortable standing in my room, and once again I wonder if I can really do this. Can I chain my future to someone who can't even be in the same room as me?

Rexus clears his throat and shifts in place. I think he's about to take his leave, so

I'm shocked when he says; "Would you like help to shower?"

"More than anything. Mostly because I'm not sure my legs will hold me." He nods and toes off his shoes, which he'd left untied. His pants go next, and my eyes can't help but wander to his cocks. They're still impressive, even when flaccid.

"I'd thought as much. My own shower was a battle." He disappears into the bathroom, and a moment later, the shower cuts on. It's another long moment before he reappears.

He steps forward and pulls the blanket off me and pauses with his hands out. "May I?"

So, I'm not the only one feeling awkward. I'm actually comforted by that fact. I liked being together in our weirdness.

At my nod, Rexus slides his arms under my back and legs, then scoops me up into his arms. Warm steam fills the bathroom as he carries me inside. I inhale deeply, already feeling a bit better.

"It's warmer than I normally like. Please let me know if you need me to adjust the water." I brace for the heat as he steps into the shower. Instead, I'm hit by lukewarm temperatures.

"Do you bathe in cold water?" I squeak, snuggling closer to his body. He's no warmer than the water.

Rexus chuckles as he slowly lowers my legs until I'm standing on the cool tile. "I am cold-blooded. Cool water is optimal for comfort."

I would kill for a hot shower right now but I don't think I can manage it on my own so I resign myself to the water temp and allow Rexus to take most of my weight in one arm as he reaches around me to the shampoo.

His movements are quick and efficient as he massages it into my hair. The pressure on my scalp feels amazing, though I'm loathing trying to brush the tangles free.

Rexus angles me back under the spray and helps me rinse the shampoo from my hair. His fingers work through some of the smaller snarls as I wallow in the water. It's too soon before he's pulling me out from under the spray again.

"Can you stand on your own?" I test my weight and think I probably can. At my nod, he pulls away, leaving one hand on my waist. He puts his hand under the dispenser on the wall, and the sweet smell of vanilla fills the room as body wash pools into his hand.

I wonder yet again why the aliens stocked everything vanilla scented and pink and fluffy. Who was on the human informant team when they decided what human women liked? Elle Woods?

His hands are gentle as he smooths the soap over me. Up my arms, down my sides. He's perfunctory when washing my tits but slows down over the curve of my belly. I would have thought it impossible to get aroused again, but pleasure pools in my belly as he moves his hands around and up to wash my back.

After getting more body wash, he drops to a knee to wash my legs, stopping just at the top of my thighs. I spread my feet to give him access but he just eyes me warily.

"Rexus?" At his name, he looks up at me with something like regret.

"I hurt you." His hand comes up to gently cup between my legs. I won't lie and say I'm not tender and a little sore, but no damage done.

I grab his hand and tangle our fingers together until I can pull him to his feet. His face is solemn as he looks down at me. For the first time, I really pay attention to our height difference. He's at least a foot taller than me and built so strong, but he's so gentle with me.

Even in the middle of the rut, he didn't hurt me. Not really. Not in ways that could be helped. Of course, my pussy was tender and sore. He spent the better part of at least three days inside of me. Anyone would be sore after that, right?

# Chapter 17

## *Rexus*

Rosie looks up at me, and I wait for her recriminations. I deserve them. I had been too rough with the human, and now she is damaged. I damaged her.

For hours, I've been dealing with the fact I hurt her and that there was no way she would want to stay with the monster who caused her so much pain. I don't blame her. But I would give just about anything to have her stay.

Waking up with her on top of me was one of the first moments of contentment I've felt since the universe went silent. For over a year, it's just been silence and work. There was no room for anything else.

"Do aliens have titanium pussies?" She says, her eyes shut as soon as the words are out, like she didn't mean to speak them. Understandable, as they make no sense.

"I do not understand." I urge her back under the spray to wash her body free from the soap I'd slicked over her skin. An act that shouldn't have been arousing, yet I was fighting back arousal all the same.

She snorts out a laugh. "How long were we fucking? Days? A week? Of course my pussy is rubbed raw. But you didn't hurt me. It aches but it doesn't hurt."

Rosie takes my hand in hers and brings it back to cup her pussy. The flesh is so soft and warm beneath my fingers. I fight the urge to pet her. To spread her folds and brush my fingers through them. To delve my fingers inside her wet heat.

Instead, I just cup her, feeling the heat of her flesh against my hand and the weight of her hand encircling my wrist to keep me in place.

"I'm not broken," she says, releasing my wrist to slide her hand up my arm until she's gripping my shoulders. I can't help but press my fingers in deeper, to get a touch of her warmth. She gasps, and her head falls back.

Water runs down her body, and I can't stop myself from tracing a drop down the curve of her breast before sucking it off the pointed tip. Her grip on my shoulders tightens as I suck the wide brown nipple into my mouth.

There is no reason I should want her again so soon. It's irrational, this need inside of me to touch her. But I can't stop myself from sucking harder or from sliding one finger inside the clasp of her body.

Nails dig into my shoulders as I gently work my way inside her. The tiny points of pain only flame the fire of my need. My cocks are hard against her stomach. She arches against them, and I know there's no way we're leaving this shower without me getting inside of her.

I pull my finger free to the sound of her whine. I grip her hips and lift her until I can slide her pussy against my cocks.

"Tell me no," I tell her, pushing her back against the tiled wall. I align one of my cocks at her entrance. "Tell me to stop."

"Please, Rexus." She squirms in my grasp until the tip of my cock is caught in the tight clench of her body. The flare presses up against the outside of her body, and it's more than I can handle, not being inside of her.

Still, I'm careful as I work myself into

her body. She's so tight, and the clench of her is impossible to stand. My legs shake as pleasure pools deep inside of me. I thrust until I'm fully seated only to pull her off my cock entirely and swap her to my second one.

I can't help but feel like this is the last time I'll get to be inside of her, and I want to feel her on both cocks. Short, slow thrusts that have my legs shaking and my arms straining as I work her up.

In this position, there's no way to work the little bundle of nerves that brings her such pleasure, so I pull out and change cocks again until I have one inside of her and one pressed between our bodies. I shift until my second cock is nestled between her splayed lips.

"Fuck, Rexus. Yes." Her nails dig into my shoulders as her legs tighten around my waist. When her back arches, I take advantage and duck my head to suck one of her nipples into my mouth.

Her breathing picks up along with my movements. I release her nipple and press her harder into the tiles as I begin to slide her up and down my cock, meeting her body with every thrust.

"I can't, oh, god."

Rage fills me at the sound of another's name. "Who is this god? He is not inside of you. I am. If you're going to scream anyone's name while I'm fucking you, it's going to be mine."

She laughs until I thrust into her with all my strength, showing her who she belongs to in this moment. The sound becomes a scream as I begin to fuck her with a punishing pace. I want to fuck her until she forgets any male that came before me. Until I ruin her for any male that may come after me.

Another spike of anger at the thought of this little human with another male. I press my fingers into her flesh, wanting to leave my mark on her. She is mine. And while I have no right to claim her, I have every intention of keeping her.

# Chapter 18

## *Rosie*

I have every expectation of Rexus leaving as soon as we come down from our post-orgasm high. It fits with what he's shown me previously, so I'm a little shocked when he carefully lowers me to the ground before washing me again. As soon as we're both clean, he bundles me into a towel and carries me out to the living room.

"I'm going to change the bedding," he says after settling me on the couch and leaving me with another cup of water. Pickles climbs up onto the couch beside me and gives me a look.

"Yeah, I don't know either," I tell the possum. I scratch behind its ears a little, and it bumps its head into my touch. "I'll get you some proper food in a little bit."

Headquarters had given us a large

supply of kibble for the possum that was in an automatic feeder, but based on research, she needed fresh produce and protein sources as well. Something I hadn't had time for the last few days. The poor thing had tried to join me on the bed at one point only to be scared off by Rexus waking up to fuck me again. I hadn't seen her until now.

We stay like that for a few moments before Rexus returns with a large bundle of blankets and sheets, all of which would have to be washed before I could touch them again. I could smell the stench of sex and sweat coming off them from here.

"I'm going to get these to the laundry." It's only then that I notice he's gotten dressed and is wearing his boots again. He shuffles his feet a little before asking, "Do you need anything?"

"No, I'm good." And it's almost entirely true.

I don't allow myself to couch rot for long before I get up and get dressed in a pair of loose sweats and a cropped boxy tee. I feed

Pickles and myself lettuce wraps with some kind of meat that tastes almost like beef. Almost.

After spending thirty minutes working every last snarl out of my hair, I secure it back in a braid. It's only half dry, but it'll have to do.

Grabbing my communicator from the end table, I settle back onto the couch with a blanket and a cup of steaming tea. I open the novel I always thought I would write and read through the few scenes I've managed so far.

I'd started planning this book when I was in undergrad, always promising myself I would write it one day. One day, after school was over. One day, when I had time. One day, it will be finished. And yet, sitting there, I feel no passion for it. I realize I just don't care about the characters, about the story.

Closing the file, I open a new one. A blank page. A completely new beginning.

Maybe it isn't what I planned. I'd certainly planned on being with Betty forever, until she realized she too preferred dick. I'd planned to have my mom long into old age, until she died at fifty. I'd never imagined finding aliens in my timeline. And yet here

I am, on an alien planet fucking a lizard-like alien with a million abs and an inability to be in a room with me outside of fucking.

And isn't that a kick in the teeth? The male is my only point of contact on this rock and, other than fucking me, doesn't want to spend any time with me. I'd thought it would be okay. Other than Betty, I haven't had a successful relationship in my life. I am very used to being alone. I'm not used to being lonely.

I have just over two months before I have to decide if I stay on Planet WLN269 or if I go home. If I go home, I lose the bulk of the payout. I'll be back where I started.

But can I stay on a planet with someone who only wants me for what's between my legs? Until I can make that decision, I need to stay away from Rexus. Because whenever he's near, I want impossible things.

# Chapter 19

## *Rexus*

"How's domestic life?" Kan-RI asks me as we patrol the perimeter of the village together. He and I have worked together many years, and he is the closest thing I have to a friend. The male is much shorter than me, but the black tipped yellow plumes on the top of his head give him the impression of height. His beak and eyes are stark black against bright yellow feathers. His hands tucked into his pockets, giving the impression of casual. Though he is one of the most dangerous males I've ever met.

"Complicated," I tell him. I'm not certain I want to discuss my relationship with Rosie. It feels private, and I do not want to shame her. But I would also love to get another male's perspective.

"Inter-species relationships are always a little bit complicated." Kan-RI says sagely. He is in a long-term pleasure partnership with one of the gardeners in the village so he has an idea of it, I suppose. But I do not think it's quite the same.

At least his partner is stuck here. There isn't a clock ticking down the time until he's given a chance to leave. He doesn't have to be concerned he will be left behind again.

"She is only fulfilling the terms of our agreement." I say, trying not to taste the bitter words on my tongue. I'd wanted someone who did not wish to have a romantic relationship, someone who would be fine on their own. I'm the one unable to uphold our agreement.

"How do you mean?" Kan-RI asks, tilting his head as he looks up at me. "Oh, Rexus, what did you do?"

I'm silent as we continue our patrol, uncertain I want to tell him how stupid I'd been. How had I thought I would be able to feel absolutely nothing for someone who could take my rut so well? Then again, I hadn't known she would be so soft. So lovely. So perfect in my grip.

"This is about Seela, isn't it?" Kan-RI asks as we near the gatehouse. I want to deny it, but it would be a lie. "It's okay to miss her, friend."

Of course I missed Seela. We had been fuck friends for many years. Her heat had perfectly matched my rut and we'd been able to give each other what we needed. She'd been a fierce female and my partner for many years. We'd come to Planet WL-N269 together, worked together, fucked together. But we were not in love. For us, it was never anything but friendship and physical release.

But I'd lost a part of myself when the worlds went silent and she did not return from a trip back home. It was a relationship I did not know how to replace. One I wasn't sure would be possible to have again. I did not know if I was able to open myself up again, knowing that people can so easily be torn away.

I think about lying. I think about telling him she has nothing to do with it. But we'd all lost people when the worlds went silent. We'd all known that pain.

"She could leave me." I tell him. We stop outside of the gatehouse, just out of earshot of the guards inside. "It's only a matter of weeks until she is given the choice to go home. I do not know why she would stay."

I don't tell him how I hurt her. I do not tell him about my rut or my fear of touching her for causing her pain. My shame is too large and I do not want to discuss Rosie that way.

"What if she doesn't leave? What if you give her a reason to stay?" He pats me on my arm and takes off for the gatehouse, leaving me standing in the yard with my mind buzzing and my heart racing.

A thought I haven't allowed myself to consider since the moment I came out of my rut turns over and over.

What if she stays?

# Chapter 20

## *Rosie*

I read the message on my communicator for the second time and lean back against the back of the couch as the meaning settles around me. I have options. And that's almost as terrifying as not having any.

According to the H.E.L.P. agent, I could stay on WLN269 without having to stay with Rexus. I could keep my apartment and be matched with someone new. They did say they couldn't promise I'd stay in Village 22 but I didn't think I'd want to stay here anyway.

I'd still get the full payment at the end of the three months, which would take care of all of my debt on Earth plus leave some money leftover for emergencies. Or I could go home, get a third of the settlement money, which would give me a small bit of breathing room before I had to find a job. But I'd be back to sleeping in Betty and Craig's spare bedroom.

No matter what, I don't think staying with Rexus is an option. No matter how much I wish it could be.

And oh, I wish I could stay with him. He can be so sweet when he tries and he's hands down the best fuck I've ever had. But I don't think we'll ever be more than horny acquaintances and I just don't think that will be enough for me.

Not when I could accidentally find myself falling in love with him. Not when he's made it clear he isn't interested in emotional entanglements. Not when I might be halfway there already.

I toss my communicator to the side only to pick it up a moment later. I need a distraction and my novel is just the thing. Am I projecting in my book about a human falling in love with an alien? Maybe. But what is writing if not author trauma dumping on the page?

Ever since I gave myself permission to start over, the words have been flowing. I've gotten into a routine over the last week that's comfortable. It's one I could enjoy, if I didn't know it wouldn't last.

Pickle curls up beside me and nudges her nose and front paws under my leg. I give her head a couple of scratches before I dive into the story. I have a few hours yet before Rexus will be here with dinner and I need to get my head on straight before he arrives.

I lose myself in the story. In the battle of fighting alien factions, in the human trapped in space, in the romance building between her and one of the faction leaders. I let myself imagine what it would be like to be so wanted that someone would burn worlds down to keep you safe.

I'm in the middle of a particularly hot sex scene when there's a knock on the door. It slides open without me answering and Rexus walks in carrying a covered tray. I lost track of time.

Rexus' smile drops as he looks me over. "What are you up to?"

I blush and put the communicator aside. I'm sure I'm flushed and I can feel the dampness between my thighs as I shift on the couch. I'd gotten really into the story. Who could blame me? I'm a woman with a high sex drive who hasn't been fucked in a week while having dinner with an insanely hot male almost every night. Of course some good smut would get me worked up.

"Writing a book." I tell him. It's the first time I've said those words out loud in years. I'm writing a book. They taste good on my tongue.

"Interesting." He crosses the room to set the tray on the kitchen table before turning back to me. "Then why do you look and smell like you're begging to get fucked?"

I bite my lip to try to think of an answer. I hadn't realized he could smell my arousal. That was almost embarrassing. Rexus crosses the room and looms over me with his legs pressed against my crisscrossed shins and his arms caging me in as he presses his hands to the back of the couch.

"Do you want me to fuck you, Rosie?"

The smart thing would be to say no, absolutely not. It would be a complete lie but it might help me keep a clear head. We're good at fucking. We both know that. It's everything else that we suck at.

But the horny little bitch who lives inside of me speaks first. "More than anything."

# Chapter 21

## *Rexus*

Rosie shrieks as I scoop her up and toss her over my shoulder. The sound followed by a giggle as I carry her to the bedroom.

This was not my plan. My plan is to woo Rosie until she likes me enough to want to stay. To eat with her and talk to her, things the human guides say make women fall in love. But, while always nice, there is a wall around Rosie that I can't get through.

I was prepared for another polite dinner until the moment I walked into the domicile and saw her. Smelled her. She was ripe and ready, and I am a weak man. My need to be inside of her is all-consuming.

It's the only time she lets her guard down, and I can feel close to her. I'll take whatever I can get at this point. I'm desperate for her. However I can have her.

She's still laughing when I drop her onto the bed and follow her down. I prop myself up on my elbows and look down at her. The gold of her hair, the soft blue of her eyes, the pink of her lips. She's absolutely lovely.

I must stare too long because she stops laughing and her face becomes solemn. She tilts her head as our eyes meet, hold.

"What?"

"You're lovely," I tell her, brushing her hair away from her face with my hands. Her lips part on a quiet breath that rocks through me.

Before the silence can stretch on too long, I dip my head to take in her sweet scent. I dart my tongue out to taste her. She's sweet and salty under my tongue, and I want to trace it along every inch of her flesh.

I settle for tracing a path down her neck until I can close my teeth over that spot on her shoulder she likes so much. She moans and arches into me. Her hand fists on my back with her little nails digging into my flesh. I savor the pain, the connection.

I'm still licking and nibbling my way

across her shoulder and down into the curve of her breasts when she releases me and pushes against my chest. I push up onto my hands, confused.

"Off," she says, pushing again. Disappointment flares, but I climb off of her and then the bed. I'm about to make my excuses and get out of there when she reaches for my belt. "Do you ever wear a shirt?"

It takes a moment to answer when she follows the question with a press of her lips to my torso. And another, a little lower.

"My kind breathes through our skin. Shirts are suffocating." When her mouth travels lower, I grip her shoulders and stop her. "What are you doing?"

"What I want." Her grin is devilish. She pulls my belt free of the clasp and undoes my pants. My cocks are at attention as she shoves my pants over my hips. Her hand clasps them both, barely able to wrap around them enough to hold them together.

"I want to—ung!" I lose all thought as Rosie leans forward to take my first cock in her mouth. Was this something humans did? It is so obscene, but the flick of her tongue and the pressure is enough to make my knees weak.

"Get your boots off." Rosie says as she

comes off my cock. She releases me and reaches for the hem of her shirt. She's wearing nothing beneath it, and suddenly I'm faced with an expanse of soft, creamy skin. "Rexus, boots."

I sit on the bed and hurry to unlace and kick off my boots while Rosie raises up on the bed to wriggle out of her skin-tight pants. I turn my head and find myself face to pussy. It's too much to take.

Ignoring my pants, I grip her ass and pull her forward by the round globes until I can bury my face into her sweet folds. They're plump and damp under my tongue.

"Rexus! It's my turn." Rosie says, even as she allows me to pull her forward and around until she's straddling my legs and pressed firmly against my face.

"Later," I say. I lean back, bringing her with me until she's on her knees over my face. I lick and tease her all the way down.

"No, nope. I'm too heavy for this." She tries to squirm out of my grasp, but I shift to hold her hips until she's trapped right where I want her. "I'm going to suffocate you."

"That's not how I breathe, woman. Now sit on my fucking face and let me taste you." I'm desperate for it. For her.

Finally, she stops fighting me and lowers herself down until I can drown myself in the scent and feel of her. There's no finesse from this position, no slow teasing. It's just me devouring the best thing I've ever tasted.

Rosie is leaning forward with her hands planted against the wall. Her head tipped forward. Our eyes meet over the rounded curve of her belly as I feast on her. When her eyes go a little hazy, I know I've found the right spot. I settle in until I can wring every last orgasm out of her.

# Chapter 22

## *Rosie*

The third orgasm crashes through me, and I tap out. I can't take anymore. My legs are shaking to the point they're almost useless. While I may not be able to suffocate Rexus, I still don't want to put my entire weight on his face.

My pussy is clenching on nothing, and I can think of another place I'd rather be sitting. Another position I want to try. I squeeze his hands on my hips and push up as far as I can.

"Please Rexus, I need you inside of me." He grins and releases my hips. He starts to slide out from under me, but I stop him. "No, stay."

The little wriggling crawl down his body is the furthest thing from sexy, but his eyes don't leave my body. Neither do his hands. They clutch the curves of my waist as I get into position over his cocks.

"What?" His eyes are drawn but they flutter shut as I lower myself onto his top cock. The flare under his head rubs me in just the right way as I work my way down him. I lean forward until my hands are on his chest and I can work myself up and down him.

"This is a first," his eyes are half-mast as he looks up at me. "This is pleasurable for you?"

I slide down and swivel my hips until his hands grasp harder on my sides and he lets out a groan.

"Very," I tell him, rocking back and forth until I find a rhythm I enjoy. His second cock taps against my ass with every thrust of my hips, and I want it inside of me too.

He's never once tried to fuck me with both penises at the same time. Not even when he was in the height of his rut and completely out of his mind. Maybe it wasn't something his species did. Maybe he wouldn't like it.

But maybe he would.

I slide all the way down until his second cock is braced against my ass. It jumps and bumps against my hole, and I grin.

"I'm going to suggest something that might sound a little weird, and I'm okay if you don't want to do it. Just tell me it's too weird. But I want both of you cocks."

Rexus groans, and his grip tightens almost painfully. I can feel the second cock flexing against my ass. Okay, not totally disliked.

"Oh, little one, you tight hole can barely handle one cock. You are not designed to take both." Concern and disappointment war in his voice as he loosens his grasp and tries to urge me to move again.

I think about telling him about double-dick-in-pussy penetration and the size of a baby's head. But neither of those things matter, right now.

"I have two holes," I point out as I rock back against his other cock.

His eyes flash hot, which sends a wave of heat through me. Oh, yeah, he's into it.

"You did not like my contact there," he says, gritting his teeth and lifting me slightly. Off and away from his second cock.

"You surprised me, that's all. I'm not opposed to anal sex." This time, he lowers me down until his head lines up with my asshole. "Oh, ho, no. Wait!" I push against his grip and away from his cock.

"You just said-"

"I know what I said but we need some kind of lubricant." I look around the room, as if expecting some to magically appear. I certainly didn't bring any with me.

"You seem to have plenty," his fingers drag between my legs, and I shudder as they make contact with my clit.

He's not wrong. I am dripping around his cock. I've never used body fluids as lubricant before, but I've heard it can work. I slide off of him. He makes a small distressed sound that turns into a groan as I take his second cock into me. I position myself until his first cock is pressing against my clit when I lean forward and ride him.

"Fuck," he groans, gripping my hips and moving me over him. "I'm going to come from this alone."

Honestly, I'm close. So close. But it's not what I want. Not this time. Not if it's going to be our last time. And if I'm not staying, it has to be. I can't keep fucking him if I don't get to keep him. It's not fair to either of us.

I push against his chest until he releases me and I can slide off of him. His cock dripping with my fluids. I'm not sure it's enough, but it'll have to be. I shift and position myself above him. Rexus grips his front cock while I reach behind me to angle the second one.

"Keep still," I tell him as I slide down until the head and frill of his front cock is inside of my pussy. Then I lean back until I can press against his second cock.

Rexus is still as stone beneath me. His fingers flex on my thighs, but he doesn't move or force me down. I relax and bear down as the tip of his cock presses inside of me.

I gasp as Rexus groans. Neither of us move for a long moment as we adjust to the feel of him inside of me. "If you don't move soon, I'm going to lose my mind."

There's no choice, I move. I slide down his cocks until I'm so full I can hardly breathe. Rexus holds still as I try to find a comfortable rhythm, but his hands are shaking on my thighs as he struggles to let me be in control.

Sweat breaks out across my body as I set a slow, steady pace. My legs are already shaking and I'm not close. It's adrenaline, arousal, pleasure. They're all wrapped up together until I can barely manage myself.

Rexus breaks. His hands move to my hips and curl around my ass as he moves me up and down over him. I scream out as he slams me down against his body and the tip of his cock hits my cervix as the base of the other slams against the sensitive ring of flesh on my ass.

I cup my breasts as he sets a brutal pace, thrusting up into me at the same time as he slams me down. Nonsense falls from my lips as I try to keep up with him. But it's just so much. Too much.

He slams me down one last time, and I come apart around him. My body clenches his cocks so tightly that I can feel it when he releases inside of me. Every throb of his cocks sends aftershocks through me.

I collapse on his chest in a heap of sweaty, destroyed woman. Rexus is no better. His cocks slide free of me, pulling matching groans from each of us. His chest heaves beneath me as he struggles to catch his breath.

This may be our last time, but what a time it was.

# Chapter 23

## *Rosie*

I recover first, "how do you feel about dinner in bed?"

It's a bold assumption, that he won't leave like he always does. But I don't want him running out on me right now. I'm too raw with the need for connection.

I shift to get out of bed, but Rexus wraps a hand around my wrist and tugs me back. "Stay."

Confused but pleased, I shift until I'm leaning against him again. His arm goes around me and pulls me closer. I try not to let myself get used to it.

"Okay, but you're going to have to feed me eventually. I'm starving."

"No," he tilts my face up to meet his gaze. "Stay with me."

My breath catches in my chest, and my

heart is in my throat as I stare up at him. His face is solemn and sincere.

"What?" I'm so afraid I'm just hearing what I want to hear and putting too much weight into his words. That he means right now, not forever.

He can't possibly mean forever. He's the one who set the 'no emotional entanglements' rule.

"I know you have a couple more months to decide, but I'd like you to stay with me. I don't want you to go."

"What about your "romantic entanglements" rule." I need to make sure we're on the same page. I need to know he's not just asking me to stay for an easy fuck. Because, I won't survive being his escape when I want him to be my everything.

"It's a dumb rule. Very stupid. I don't know what I was thinking." He bends down to press his mouth against my head. The kiss is brief, but his eyes are bright when he pulls away. "There was someone before you."

My heart sinks. I knew there must have been but I didn't particularly want to hear about a previous woman while naked in bed together.

"Her name was Seela and she was my

best friend." He shifts and drags me closer. "We weren't lovers, but we'd help each other when one of us was in rut or heat."

"What happened to her?" Because something had definitely happened to her. I could tell now. It was in the lines of his face, the darkness in his eyes, in the fierce way he hugs me.

"She went home to visit family. She was there when the worlds went silent." I knew about the silence. It was why Earth had teamed up with WLN269 in the first place. Their entire galaxy had gone silent overnight. For a year they tried to contact anyone. But never heard back. The only people left were the 50,000 men and 1,000 women on the mining planet.

"Oh, Rexus," I wrap my arm around his torso and hug him tight. "I'm so sorry for your loss."

"It's hard to lose someone."

"My mom died last year." I tell him, "It's part of why I'm here. I spent so much time taking care of her, I forgot to take care of everything else."

"Then you can understand why I did not want to invite that pain again." He sighs and pulls me closer until I'm sprawled halfway on top of him. "But from the moment I saw you, there was no resisting you."

"Right," I laugh.

"You're lovely, so soft and warm. You smell and taste wonderful. You're kind and your pussy is the most perfect thing I've ever seen." His fingers trail down the front of me until they cup me from behind. "There is more to a relationship, of course, but I want time to learn everything about you. And I can't do that if you're leaving."

I push off of him until I'm sitting next to him. I cannot have this conversation sprawled on top of him. And I definitely can't do it with his fingers pressed against my pussy.

"You can't keep leaving me alone all the time. I get you have work and a life but I'm going crazy sitting in here all the time."

"I'd like to combine domiciles. We can use whichever you prefer." He takes my hand in his and toys with my fingers. "I do not like being away from you."

"Oh, okay." Well, that was easy. "You have to introduce me to your friends. And there was a girl on the flight up, I'd like to find her contact information. I need other contacts besides you."

"I cannot promise we'll find the human

but I shall ask Headquarters to help. I shall introduce you to Kan-RI and his partner whenever you like."

"You're being awfully accommodating." I narrow my eyes at him, not sure I can trust it.

"I want you here and I want you happy enough to stay. I will do whatever I can to make it happen. I'll probably mess it up because I've never had a mate before, so you'll need to tell me when I have and help me fix it."

"I can live with that." I lean forward and press my lips to his. "Now, can you please feed me? I'm dying over here."

# Chapter 24

## *Rexus*

"You have to let me read it," I tell Rosie. She just came into the bedroom crowing that she had finished her book. And now she insists I cannot read it. Rude.

"I have to edit it first. It's not done yet."

"But you just said—" She sets her communicator on the charging pad next to mine and launches herself on me.

"My first draft is done. I still have to edit it. Probably more than once. But I've never finished a full rough draft before." She straddles my lap and wraps her arms around my neck. "I'm excited."

"I'm proud of you." I wrap my arms around her waist and bring her closer until I can thrust my already half-hard cocks against her through my sweatpants. They're a human article of clothing that I've fallen in love with. So much softer than the durable clothing standard issue on WLN269.

For my birthday, Rosie ordered a few pairs for me after she got tired of me wearing hers and 'stretching them out' on her. It was the most thoughtful gift I've ever received.

"Ugh, what if it's bad?" She frowns, and I lean forward to kiss the expression off her face.

"It's not."

"How would you know?"

"Well, you could let me read it." She slaps my chest before hugging me close. "It's not terrible because you're brilliant and a talented story teller."

I could listen to Rosie tell me stories about her life on Earth forever. Of her explorations around WLN269. She has a way of telling them that has me hanging on every word. I have no doubt her book is much the same.

"Thank you," she snuggles against my chest, and I run my hands up and down her back until I can cup her ass. "Stop it."

"Stop what?" I slide my hands up until I can slide them under her pants and put my hands on flesh.

"Distracting me." But she's laughing as she snuggles closer to give me a better grip. I dip my fingers in until I can spread her cheeks wide.

"I would never," I say, pressing a fingertip against her puckered hole. "Are you going to tell me about it?"

She picks up her head to glare at me before she grinds down on my cocks. It seems impossible that after nearly a year my hunger for this woman has not waned in the least. Every time I'm near her, I have to be touching her.

"Next transport comes up soon. It's not too late to change your mind." I lick the top curve of her ear before biting down. "If I'm such a bother."

"You're the worst kind of bother," Rosie says, pushing up until she can haul her shirt over her head and drop it on the floor beside the bed. "And I'm not going anywhere. You're stuck with me."

I flip us until Rosie is lying on her back and I'm kneeling between her knees. "Damn right you're not. Sorry, little one, you're stuck with me."

"Oh, no. How horrible." Rosie's eyes sparkle up at me as she helps me work her pants off. "You poor male."

"Poor little human." I kick off my pants before spreading out over her body to rest my hardness against all of her soft curves. I nuzzle into her neck and take in her sweet scent that hasn't gotten less delicious over time. I still want to wallow in her.

"Oh, my god. Will you just fuck me already?" She wraps her legs around my waist and pulls me closer.

"Anything for you, mate." And, as I slide into her, it feels like coming home.

# Planet WLN269 Needs Women Series Titles:

Planet WLN269 Needs Women: A Prequel by Dakota Cockaday writing as Cassi O. Peia

Home, Home on the Strange by May Furhst

Going Batty for You by E.K. Darnell

Filling the Void While Also Being Filled by the Void by Ginger Kane

Alotl Love to Share by Holly Hanzo

Taken in by the Aliens by Sabrina Cross

Love & Other Squibbles by Kenzie James

# About the Author

Sabrina Cross (she/her) is a neurospicy 80's baby from the middle of nowhere Michigan, where she still lives with her cat. She came into her monster romance era early when she fell in love with Beast from the 1997's X-Men animated series. After discovering sentient object romance in early 2023, Sabrina decided to embrace what she calls her 'Hold My Beer' style of writing and gave into the lifelong dream of being an author. When not writing weird monster/sentient object smut, Sabrina can be found hanging out on social media (@authorsabrinacross), reading, or hoarding office supplies.

# Also by Sabrina Cross

## Yarn & Monsters Series

A True Love Spell Gone Wrong...

When four friends perform a true love spell, things go terribly wrong. Now they're locked into a deal with the devil and have only a year to find love and happiness or their souls are destined to face the flames. Armed with a demon guardian; Clover, Jasmine, Fern, and Violet are determined to beat the devil and save themselves. Except, this curse might be the best thing that's ever happened to them.

Corny: A F/F Candy Corn Romance

Snuggle: A M/F Demon Teddy Bear Romance

Tangled: A M/F Friends-To-Lovers Sentient Object Romance

Knotted: A M/F Demon Werewolf Romance

## The Cursed Matchmaker Series

Never Piss off a witch. Or else you may find yourself trapped in a glory hole booth at an upscale sex club. But when the perfect couples hook up anonymously, Josh has no choice but to speak out and help them find love.

The Glory Whole Package

The Glory Whole Experiment

The Glory Whole Redemption

**Retro Whimsy Series**

Welcome to Retro Whimsy where nothing is as it seems and the owners know just what you need.

Getting Railed

Trogg Trouble

Game Girl

**Ghostlight Falls - Shared World Series**

Cooking Up A Demon

**Planet WLN269 Needs Women - Shared World Series**

Taken in by the Aliens

Much Ado About Rutting

**Stand Alone Monster Romance**

Christmas with the Monster

Can't Yeti Enough

**Stand Alone Sentient Object Romance**

Light Me Up

Pounded by the Pommel Horse

Sentient Pen15 from Outer Space

Knotty Broomsticks